Follow Me Into the Night

By Amy Laundrie

Illustrations by Abira Das

Published by Pen It! Publications, LLC in the U.S.A.

812-371-4128 www.penitpublications.com

ISBN: 978-1-63984-046-5

Illustrated by Abira Das

Acknowledgements

Love and gratitude to illustrator extraordinaire
Abira Das, my supportive critique groups, and
encouraging friends.

"Writer Chicks on the Road"
"Women in Motion"
"Kids@Heart"
  Sharon Addy
  Cindy Schumerth

Dedication

To Jay and Mason and all those
who delight in adventure

The flashlight dimmed, flickered, and then went out. Oliver knocked it against his palm, but no luck!

Grrrr-Grrrr

"This could get scary," Paris said, creeping ahead. "Good thing we have the moonlight." Paris grabbed Oliver's arm. "Is that a bear?"

Paris caught a glimpse of something black-and-white waddling in front of them.

Paris led the way

"I think my eyes adjusted," Paris said, "I can see pretty well—Oooo! Look out, Luna."

Oliver stumbled along, passing fireflies as they hiked deeper into the woods.

Oliver's eyes watered. "What's making that rustling sound?"

Even with his eyes burning, Oliver laughed. It was cut short, though, by a spine-tingling sound.

Whip-poor-will,
whip-poor-will

"Th-that's just a night bird." he stuttered. "But maybe we should turn back."

Once across, they gave each other a high-five.
A distant light beamed from the porch.
They headed for the cabin.

Facts About Luna Moths and their Friends

 * Lunas have two fake owl eyes on their wings so predators such as bats and birds think they're a scary owl instead of a tasty snack.
* Luna moths only live about a week and never eat so they don't have mouths.
* Female lunas spray a musk when it's time to mate. Males can smell this alluring perfume from miles away.

 * A luna can hear a bat's ultrasonic hunting calls through its ears and antenna.
* Each night, bats can eat their body weight or more in insects like pesky mosquitoes.

 * Owls usually swallow their prey whole then regurgitate (throw up) pellets of undigestible bones, fur, and feathers.

 * Raccoon moms try to keep their kits safe in dens. Once they're two or three months old, though, the kits want to explore. At six months, they're ready to go out on their own.

 * A skunk can have its scent glands removed. Some people enjoy keeping these clever, curious critters as pets.

* Fireflies aren't flies, but winged beetles. Not all have the ability to light up.

 * Flying squirrels don't actually fly, but they sure can glide!

Facts About Luna Moths and their Friends

 * Opossums deserve our thanks for acting as nature's trash collectors. They're omnivores and eat almost anything including ticks and slugs.

 * Eastern Whip-poor-wills lay their eggs so that they hatch on average 10 days before a full moon. When the moon is near full, the adults can hunt all night and bring many insects back to their young.

 * The term for animals who are active at night is nocturnal.

Fun Things to Do

For examples of night games, a cool experiment, and printable activities such as a scavenger hunt, word find, crossword puzzle, and maze, visit http://laundrie.com/teachers.

Amy Laundrie, a retired teacher and the author of nine other books, grew up playing "Ghost in the Graveyard," an outdoor nighttime hide-and-seek game. She's anticipating her upcoming "sleep out under the stars" night and hopes to see some of the nocturnal animals featured in this book—with the exception of the skunk. Check out the special night games and fun activities listed in the teacher section of her website at www.laundrie.com.

Lightning Source UK Ltd.
Milton Keynes UK
UKHW051500200821
389156UK00002B/13